Here is a list of words that might make it easier
to read this book. You'll find them in boldface
the first time they appear in the story.

Hawaii	huh-WO-ee
Volcanoes	vol-KAY-nohz
Nawahi	nuh-WO-hee
Kapua	ko-POO-uh
Kilauea	kee-lou-AY-uh
Mihana	mee-HON-uh
Pualani	poo-uh-LON-ee
hula	HOO-luh
macadamia	ma-kuh-DAY-mee-uh
orchids	OR-kuhds
squawked	skwawkt
extinguisher	ik-STING-gwi-sher
conclusions	kuhn-KLOO-zhunz
poisonous	POI-zuhn-us
anonymously	ah-NO-nuh-muhs-lee
lei	lay

Barbie

The Legend of the Pink Pearl

BARBIE and associated trademarks are owned by and used under license from Mattel, Inc. © 1999 Mattel, Inc. All Rights Reserved. Published by Grolier Books, a division of Grolier Enterprises, Inc. Story by Linda Williams Aber. Photo crew: Joe Atlas, Patrick Kittel, Susan Kurtz, Robert Holley, and Judy Tsuno. Produced by Bumpy Slide Books. Printed in the United States of America.

ISBN: 0-7172-8859-5

GROLIER
B O O K S

Chapter One

Barbie checked the controls on the small, twin-engine plane.

"Looks good, Kira!" she called to her friend. "We'll be ready for takeoff in just a few minutes!"

Barbie worked as a pilot for the Island Flight Seeing Tour Company. Living and working on the Big Island of **Hawaii** was a dream come true. Barbie loved the thrill of flying over **Volcanoes** National Park. And she loved sharing the sight with visitors.

"This should be fun!" Kira said as she settled into the passenger seat. "Thanks for the favor."

"No problem!" Barbie replied. "But what is this special package you have to pick up?"

Kira smiled proudly. "Kim **Nawahi,** the director of the Volcano Art Center, is sending me to pick up the Pink Pearl."

"The Pink Pearl!" Barbie exclaimed. "The one from the old Hawaiian legend?"

Kira nodded. "It's part of a traveling exhibit that's coming to the Art Center. Right now, it's on the other side of the island being cleaned and examined. I'm bringing it back for the exhibit's opening."

"Wow!" Barbie cried. "I didn't know I'd be flying the Pink Pearl Express!"

Barbie adjusted her headset. "Preparing for takeoff," she radioed in to the control tower.

As she was about to start the engines, Barbie saw her boss, Mr. **Kapua,** waving to her from the side of the runway. Barbie opened her window and leaned out. "What's up, Mr. Kapua?" she asked.

A jolly man in a flowered shirt hurried toward the plane. "You've got two more passengers," he said. "A Mr. and Mrs. Whitestone wanted to take the tour. They said this is the only time they can make it."

"Do they know that we'll have a stopover?" Barbie asked.

"They know," Mr. Kapua answered. "In fact, when I told them about it, they seemed even more interested in taking the flight."

Before Barbie could ask more, an older couple walked over to the plane. The woman wore a white dress and matching hat. The man wore a white linen suit and a white straw hat and carried a white cane with a gold handle.

"Do you think if their last name were *Bluestone,* they'd be dressed all in blue?" Kira joked.

Barbie laughed. "I don't know about that," she said, "but I wonder why he needs the cane. He seems pretty steady on his feet."

Just then, Mr. Whitestone lifted his cane and rapped on the plane's door. "We're waiting," he said impatiently.

"I guess it's his door knocker," Kira whispered, giggling.

Barbie opened the door and unfolded the stairs. Then she offered Mrs. Whitestone a hand. As Mr. Whitestone followed, Barbie offered to hold his cane.

"No, you don't!" Mr. Whitestone snapped.

"I'll hold the cane, and you fly the plane!"

Kira and Barbie exchanged surprised glances.

"He's a little nervous about flying," Mrs. Whitestone explained.

"I understand," Barbie smiled, closing the door. "But once we're up, you'll forget about being nervous. You're in for a real treat!"

The plane lifted into the air. Mr. Whitestone gripped his cane tightly. Barbie spoke into her headset microphone, pointing out the sights below. "On our way over to the Crater Rim Trail, you'll see one of Volcanoes National Park's most mysterious sights. It's a natural wonder we call Sulphur Banks," Barbie explained.

Kira pressed her face to the window and looked down to see white vapor steaming out of cracks in a ledge.

"As we fly over Sulphur Banks, you may want to hold your nose," Barbie warned. "Those white fumes may look like cottony clouds. But they smell like a misty mass of rotten eggs!"

The Whitestones weren't listening. Seconds later, they were holding their noses and moaning. "Horrible stench!" Mr. Whitestone wailed.

"Awful!" his wife agreed.

"I warned you," Barbie laughed, steering the

plane away from the fumes. She headed for the main event of the flight-seeing tour, the volcano!

The Whitestones finally dared to breathe again. This time the air was fresh. Barbie continued talking.

"We're in luck," she said. "The **Kilauea** Volcano has decided to show us her stuff today. She's erupting!"

Even the Whitestones

paid attention now. Far below the plane, red-hot lava streamed out of a steaming crack in the earth. As Barbie made a second pass over Kilauea, she told the Whitestones more about Volcanoes National Park. "In addition to its record-setting erupting volcano, the park is known for its hiking trails, campgrounds, Crater Rim—" she explained.

"Yes, yes, very interesting," Mr. Whitestone

interrupted. "But when are we landing? We want to see the Pink Pearl."

"Oh! You've heard of the Pink Pearl?" Kira asked, surprised.

Mr. Whitestone opened his mouth to answer but quickly closed it again as the plane turned sharply to the left. Soon Barbie was lowering the landing gear. A woman in a white lab coat was waiting near the runway when they landed.

"Aloha! You're right on time!" a smiling woman said as Barbie and Kira stepped out of the plane. The Whitestones followed.

"Aloha, **Mihana,**" Kira greeted her friend. The two had worked together on many exhibits. "I wouldn't be late for the Pink Pearl. Everybody at the Art Center is waiting to see it!"

Everyone gathered around Mihana to get a look at the pearl. To their great disappointment, it was packed safely in a wooden case.

"I think it is best to keep the Pink Pearl in

the box until you reach the Art Center," Mihana suggested. "A pearl is a very small thing, and it's very easily lost."

"What?" Mr. Whitestone growled. "We risked our lives to fly over here just to see it!"

Mrs. Whitestone put her hand on her husband's arm. Mr. Whitestone sighed and looked away.

Barbie was puzzled by the Whitestones' behavior. But there wasn't time to think about it now. "I'm sorry to hurry you," she said, "but we should get back."

Kira nodded. "I have to get this back to the Art Center by five. They need to prepare for tonight's opening party." Kira thanked Mihana for examining the Pink Pearl to make sure it was the real thing.

"It was my pleasure," Mihana said. "I'm lucky to see such a cultural treasure up close."

Mr. Whitestone frowned. "If it's such a

treasure, why is it being transported on a tourist plane?" he asked.

"Oh, the Pink Pearl doesn't have much value in terms of money," Mihana explained. "It has several marks on it. But those marks, or flaws, are what help us identify it."

"The real value in the pearl lies in its legend," Kira added. "The legend says that the one who holds the Pink Pearl carries the key to perfect health!"

"Let me see it!" Mr. Whitestone said, reaching for the box.

Kira pulled the box closer to her. "Mr. Whitestone," she said, "if you wish to see the Pink Pearl, you are welcome to come to the opening at the Art Center tonight. The pearl will be on display then."

"And Noni **Pualani** will be a special guest," Mihana added. "She's famous all over the islands for her storytelling."

"She'll explain the legend of the Pink Pearl," Kira continued. "She'll also lead a **hula** dance that tells the pearl's story. I hope you'll both come," she said politely to the Whitestones.

Mrs. Whitestone whispered something to her husband.

"Thank you for the invitation," answered Mr. Whitestone, "but we'll be too tired to come to that reception tonight. We'll just come with you now when you drop off the pearl."

"I guess that would be all right," Kira said.

When the plane arrived back on the other side of the island, Barbie and Kira led the way to the Art Center. The Whitestones followed close behind.

Kira held the Pink Pearl tightly and thought, "I'll be glad when this is safe in the center!"

Chapter Two

"You're back!" a pretty Hawaiian woman greeted Kira and Barbie. "And you have the Pink Pearl, yes?"

"We sure do," Kira said, holding up the wooden box. "Barbie got us there right on time."

"And I see you've brought guests as well," Kim Nawahi said, smiling at the Whitestones. "I'm afraid the party for the opening won't be starting for a little while. As you can see, we're still getting ready."

Kim pointed to the waiters nearby. They were filling platters with fresh fruits, a bowl with

white **macadamia** nuts, and another bowl with
punch. Sweet smells of **orchids** filled the air.

"Oh, Kim!" Barbie
smiled. "Everything looks
and smells beautiful!"

Then a cheery voice
rang out from across the
room, "Aloha, Kim!"

"Noni!" Kim exclaimed.

"That's Noni Pualani," Kira explained,
pointing out the older Hawaiian woman. "We're
so lucky to have her here. It's unusual for her to
visit the Big Island. She has come here to meet
her granddaughter, who will be flying in from
California. I hope the little girl will be well
enough."

"Is she sick?" Barbie asked.

"Yes," Kira answered. "She's been very sick
lately. The doctors don't know what's wrong with
her. They're hoping the fresh island air will do

her some good."

"Well," sniffed Mr. Whitestone, "keep her away from Sulphur Banks! I'm still recovering from that unpleasant experience!"

"Perhaps some rest before the reception tonight would help you, Mr. Whitestone," Barbie suggested. "Maybe you could come back then."

Before he could answer, there was a knock at the front door. Kira went to answer it. To her surprise, the door swung open.

"Captain Sanders, Captain Sanders!" a green parrot **squawked.** The parrot sat on the shoulder of an older man in a sailor's jacket and cap.

"That's me!" the man said, tipping his sailor cap. "I'm tonight's entertainment! Perkins and me, that is!"

"Excuse me, please," Kim said to Noni. She went to the door. "Captain Sanders, is it?" she asked. "I'm afraid there's been a misunderstanding. We already have a speaker for tonight."

"But do you have someone who can tell you about the Pink Pearl?" asked Captain Sanders.

Before Kim could answer, Perkins squawked, "Captain's pearl! Captain's pearl!"

All eyes turned toward the captain as he stuffed a cracker into the bird's mouth. "Always talking, Perkins is," he laughed nervously. "But when you've got a bird that can count, you just have to put up with the noise, I guess!"

"A bird that counts?" Mrs. Whitestone asked suspiciously. "I'll believe it when I see it!"

Just then the parrot swooped toward the refreshment table and stuck his beak into a bowl. He returned to Captain Sanders and dropped two nuts into a pouch on the captain's belt. "One! Two!" the bird squawked. He flew back to the bowl for more nuts. "Three! Four!"

Perkins had counted eight nuts before Kim could stop him. "I'm sorry, Captain Sanders. Your bird is quite talented, but we don't need entertainment tonight."

"Well, then," the captain said, "I guess we'll be going. Before I leave, can't I just have a peek at the Pink Pearl?"

Mrs. Whitestone spoke up. "Yes, we'd like to see the Pink Pearl, too."

Mr. Whitestone added, "We're too tired to come back again tonight."

Kim hesitated. "Well," she finally said, "I guess I have to open the box anyway. Let's all have a look!"

Everyone moved in closer. Carefully, Kim put the wooden box down on the table and opened it up. They gasped at the beauty of the rose-colored pearl.

"I've never seen anything like it!" Mrs. Whitestone declared. "Too bad it's flawed."

Even Perkins seemed excited. He started flapping his wings on Captain Sanders's shoulder, which sent Mrs. Whitestone's hat flying.

Mrs. Whitestone began waving her arms at the bird. "Get away from me, you horrible creature!" she shouted.

The startled bird flapped away from Mrs. Whitestone. As he dodged her angry waves, Perkins knocked over a lit candle!

Suddenly Barbie cried, "The napkins are on fire!"

Everyone moved at once. Kira ran for a fire **extinguisher.** Kim pushed a nearby stack of napkins away from the flames. Mr. Whitestone tucked his cane under his arm, knocking a bowl off the table. Nuts rolled across the floor like a broken string of pearls. Mr. Whitestone grabbed his wife's hand and pulled her toward the door.

Perkins squawked, "Help!" as he flew to the captain. "Nine—"

"911!" shouted Kim. "I'll call 911!"

Thinking quickly, Barbie grabbed the punch bowl and emptied it over the fire. "It's all right now," she called. "The fire is out!"

Kim leaned on the dripping table. "Thank you, Barbie," she said. She turned to close the Pink Pearl's wooden box. Suddenly she stopped. Her hand flew to her mouth. "The Pink Pearl is missing!" she gasped.

Chapter Three

Kim was shaken. "Quickly! Everyone must look for the Pink Pearl!" she cried. "It has to be here somewhere! Check everywhere!"

Barbie and Kira got down on their hands and knees and crawled under the table. Kim and Noni both started sweeping the floor with their hands. The Whitestones quietly moved toward the door. They were halfway to it when Mrs. Whitestone slipped on a nut and fell.

"My goodness!" she gasped. Her husband helped her up and led her to a chair.

"I found it!" Kira shouted from under

the refreshment table.

"I found it!" Perkins squawked. He swooped across the room. "I found it!"

The parrot's squawking upset Kim even more. "Please, Captain Sanders," she said sternly. "You must take your bird and leave immediately. There is too much confusion as it is."

The captain grabbed Perkins and hurried out the door.

Barbie, Noni, and Kim rushed to see what Kira was holding up.

"Oh, no!" Kira cried. "It's not the Pink Pearl after all. It's just another nut!"

The group continued to search. But the pearl was gone.

"We should call the police," Kim said finally.

"No one should leave," declared Kira, looking at the Whitestones.

"Oh, no!" cried Barbie. "Captain Sanders!"

Quickly she ran to the door to see if he was

still around. But the captain and his parrot were nowhere in sight.

Soon a police officer arrived. As the director, Kim explained to him what had happened.

"And I'm afraid I've done something very silly," she added sadly. "I asked Captain Sanders and his parrot to leave!"

"Well, ma'am," the police officer said, "a man with a parrot on his shoulder shouldn't be too hard to spot. We'll find him."

"Oh, dear," Kim sighed. "Our opening reception is over before it even began!" She turned to Noni, Kira, and Barbie. "We can't have the exhibit without the Pink Pearl."

The police officer questioned everyone. Each told the story as he or she had seen it. When Mr. Whitestone's turn came, Barbie thought that he looked nervous. "We're just tourists," he insisted. "We only became interested in the Pink Pearl when we heard about it this morning."

"Yes," Mrs. Whitestone agreed. "And I certainly don't need any more pearls. I have plenty of jewelry already. Besides, we heard that the Pink Pearl has no real value."

The elderly storyteller stepped forward and gently corrected Mrs. Whitestone. "The Pink Pearl has great value among those who believe in its power for good health," Noni explained. "Why, if my own granddaughter had the Pink Pearl right now, I believe she'd get well."

The police officer looked up from his notebook. "Mrs. Pualani," he said, "did you see where the pearl went?"

"No!" Noni quickly replied. "No, of course not! That bird was causing such a fuss, it was hard to see anything!"

The police officer took down the addresses where everyone was staying. "You can all expect further questions soon," he said. "There may be searches as well."

Out of the corner of her eye, Barbie saw the Whitestones exchange worried looks.

"Oh," the police officer continued, "one more thing. You may leave here now, but I'd like you to stay on the island until this case is solved."

With that request, the officer left. The Whitestones soon followed, stepping carefully across the floor.

Kira clutched Barbie's arm. "I just know the Whitestones did it!" she hissed. "But I guess we're all suspects now. Any of us could have taken the pearl."

"You're right," Barbie whispered back. "That's exactly why we must solve the case! But let's not jump to **conclusions.**" Barbie thought for a moment. "Did you take the pearl?" she asked Kira.

Kira looked shocked. "No!"

"Me, neither," Barbie said. "That's two suspects off the list."

"And I've known Kim for years," Kira

added. "I'm sure she didn't do it."

"That leaves the Whitestones, Noni, and Captain Sanders," Barbie said.

"You really don't think that Noni took the Pink Pearl, do you?" asked Kira.

Barbie shook her head. "I don't know," she answered sadly. "Remember what Noni said about her granddaughter? She believes the pearl would make her well."

Kira sighed.

"Let's go over what happened again," Barbie said. "Maybe we'll remember something else."

Barbie and Kira compared stories. Both recalled the trouble starting when Perkins knocked over the lit candle.

"But it was Mrs. Whitestone who pushed the bird toward the table," Kira pointed out.

"That's true," Barbie agreed. "And Mr. Whitestone didn't even try to help put the fire out. He just grabbed his wife's hand and headed

25

for the door. He didn't even use his cane."

"Well, no, he did use his cane," Kira corrected. "He used it to knock over the bowl of nuts!"

"Hmmm," said Barbie. "Didn't the Whitestones look worried when the police talked about a possible search?"

"That's right!" Kira exclaimed.

"What's right?" asked Kim, coming up behind them. "Have you discovered something?"

"No, I'm afraid not," Barbie replied. "We were just comparing notes."

Kim sighed. "I just heard from the board of directors. They are blaming me for losing the Pink Pearl!"

Tears welled up in Kim's eyes. Kira put a comforting arm around her shoulders.

"Please don't worry," Barbie told Kim. "We'll do everything we can to help you find the Pink Pearl."

Chapter Four

"It is a sad day," said Noni as she followed Barbie, Kira, and Kim out of the center. "The legend of the Pink Pearl goes back hundreds of years. The pearl was lost once. It would be terrible if it were lost again."

"What do you mean?" Barbie asked.

"You must hear the legend to understand," the older woman explained.

"Would you tell it now, Noni?" Kira asked.

Noni's eyes brightened. "It would be my great pleasure. Please sit in this courtyard and listen."

Barbie, Kira, and Kim sat down on a bench

under a spreading palm tree. With a graceful motion of her arms, Noni began her story.

"Hundreds of years ago on this island, there was a lovely princess called Loki Lani. Her name means "red rose."

"One day the princess saw a beautiful flower she had never seen before," Noni continued. "She could not resist its lovely fragrance, so she drank the nectar from it. The flower tasted sweet, but it was **poisonous.** The princess immediately fell sick.

"Her father, the king, called on all the medicine men to cure his daughter. Nothing worked. At last a simple young fisherman from the village brought her a rose-colored pearl. He had found it among some oysters. He claimed that a voice from the sea had told him this pink pearl had great healing powers. It saved the princess. Soon after, the princess and the fisherman married. They lived together in health and happiness.

"Years later the pearl disappeared. After a

while, some people said that the pearl had been just a legend. But then as mysteriously as it had disappeared, it was found again. About thirty years ago, a sailor donated it to a museum. Now the Pink Pearl is part of an exhibit that travels so its story may be passed on to the people."

"Are there any recent stories of healings connected with the Pink Pearl?" Kim asked.

A sad look came over the older woman's face. "I know of no recent stories. My hope was that some of the pearl's power would help my granddaughter," she added, almost to herself. Then she seemed to remember the others listening to her. "But that was just a grandmother's dream."

"I'll walk you back to your hotel, Noni," suggested Kim.

As Barbie and Kira watched them go, Barbie did not want to think her next thought. But there it was: "Had Noni taken the pearl for her granddaughter?"

Chapter Five

It was a restless night for Barbie, filled with too many thoughts of too many suspects. She was glad to awaken to a bright blue Hawaiian sky.

Barbie went to meet Kira for breakfast at a local hotel. The two friends sat down at a table with a view of the hotel lobby.

"Look!" cried Barbie. "It's the Whitestones!"

"They're leaving!" Kira exclaimed, pointing to a pile of suitcases loaded onto a cart. Mrs. Whitestone stood by the cart while Mr. Whitestone, holding his cane, talked with the desk manager.

"Wait here," Barbie told Kira. "They haven't

seen us yet. I'll pretend I'm looking for you and just happen to bump into them."

Kira watched the scene from behind her menu.

Barbie walked around a potted palm tree as if she'd just come in through the main door. "Good morning!" she said to the Whitestones. "How nice to see you again! I'm meeting Kira for breakfast. Would you care to join us?"

Mrs. Whitestone stammered, "Oh, er, we're in a hurry this morning. I'm afraid we have no time to chat. We're leaving—"

"On a bus tour," Mr. Whitestone cut in.

"Ah, yes," Mrs. Whitestone said as Kira joined them. "That's it. We're taking a bus tour."

"But surely you're not taking all your suitcases on a tour, are you?" Kira asked. "And you can't be leaving. After all, the police said—"

"Listen," Mr. Whitestone snapped, "we don't need to talk to you!" He grabbed their cart and hurried for the main door. Mrs. Whitestone was right behind him.

In his rush to fit the cart through the door, Mr. Whitestone banged his cane on the cart. Barbie and Kira were shocked to see the handle of the cane pop open. Three perfect gems rolled out!

Mr. Whitestone quickly scooped up the gemstones and dropped them into his pocket. He glanced around, hoping no one had seen him.

"I'm calling the police!" cried Kira.

"No! Let me explain," Mr. Whitestone began. He wheeled the cart to a corner of the lobby.

Mrs. Whitestone pleaded, "You must believe us! These jewels are ours."

"We are rare-jewel buyers," explained Mr. Whitestone. "We came to Hawaii to buy these three gems. I have the receipt right here."

"We were interested in seeing the Pink Pearl, of course," Mrs. Whitestone added. "But we would never steal it. We're not thieves!"

"Then why were you running away?" Barbie asked.

"And why do you keep the gems inside your cane?" Kira wondered.

Mr. Whitestone explained, "I don't trust hotel safes. Since my cane never leaves my side, it's the safest place."

"And when the Pink Pearl disappeared," Mrs. Whitestone continued, "the police said they might search our room. We were afraid they'd find these gems and think we stole the pearl! We cannot afford to be delayed. We're meeting a gem buyer in San Francisco in two days."

Barbie wanted to believe them. But one thing still bothered her. "Mrs. Whitestone, this all started when you pushed the bird away at the Art Center."

"But you would have done the same thing!"
Mrs. Whitestone insisted. "That horrible creature
was flapping his wings right in my face!"

"Yes," Barbie had to agree. "I suppose it was
a natural reaction. But you can't leave the island.
If your story is true, the police will believe you. If
you run away, you'll only make everyone think
you're guilty."

Mr. Whitestone frowned, but he nodded. "I
guess you're right." He pushed the luggage cart
toward the front desk and turned to his wife. "Let's
check back in. We'll call the buyer tomorrow."

Barbie turned to Kira. "Time for breakfast?"

"We've earned it!" Kira laughed. "Two more
suspects off the list, and I'm starving!"

On their way back to the café, they heard a
familiar voice at the phone in the lobby.

"It's Noni!" Kira exclaimed. "Shall we ask
her to join us for breakfast?"

"Good idea," Barbie said, heading for the

phone. They could hear Noni's conversation clearly.

"Can you imagine how good it was to see the Pink Pearl?" Noni was saying into the phone. "The story of Princess Loki Lani reminds me of you, my little princess. If you can't come to see me, Nana Noni will come to see you. And then you'll be in the pink again and feeling better. I'm sure of it!"

"Oh, no!" Kira whispered to Barbie. "Does that mean she has the Pink Pearl?"

Barbie watched Noni hang up the phone. Noni looked concerned, but when she saw Barbie and Kira, her eyes brightened. "Aloha!" she said to them. "It is good to see two friends this morning. I have just been talking with my granddaughter. She tells me she's feeling better. But I think she's just trying to cheer her worried grandmother. So I've decided to go to California tomorrow to see her."

"Oh!" Barbie gasped. Then she thought quickly. "We came to tell you that there's a meeting tonight at the Art Center at eight o'clock."

"Meeting?" Noni repeated. "For what?"

"It's about the missing pearl," Barbie replied. "Please say you'll be there. It's very important."

Noni hesitated but nodded. "I have a few things to do today. But I will see you there tonight."

They said good-bye, and Noni left. As Barbie and Kira sat down to breakfast, Kira said, "I didn't know there was a meeting tonight."

"There wasn't," Barbie explained, "until now. I want to try to get everyone back together at the center. Then we can walk through what happened, step by step. Maybe we can solve this mystery."

After breakfast, Barbie and Kira went to the hotel's front desk. There they left a message for the Whitestones about the meeting.

As they were leaving, Kira murmured, "Oh, no! Look!" She pointed to a newspaper headline as they passed someone reading in the lobby.

Barbie read the headline out loud. *Pink Pearl Vanishes: Unhealthy Start for New Exhibit!"*

Chapter Six

As Barbie read, she noticed something strange. A pair of green wings was sticking out from behind the newspaper. Barbie peered over the paper. "Captain Sanders!" she exclaimed. "And Perkins! The police are looking for you."

"Captain's pearl! Captain's pearl!" the parrot squawked.

"Where's the pearl, Captain?" Kira demanded.

"I didn't steal it!" the captain shouted. "I was trying to find it again."

"I think you have some explaining to do, Captain," Barbie said.

"All right. All right," the captain mumbled. "I was trying to tell my story the other night at the Art Center. That's why I was there!"

"Well, we're listening now," said Kira.

Barbie and Kira sat down. With Perkins on his shoulder, the captain began his tale.

"About thirty years ago, Perkins and I stopped in a little jewelry store. It was mostly filled with junk jewelry. I poked around and came across a pretty-looking pearl."

"The Pink Pearl?" asked Kira.

"That's right," the captain replied. "The owner of the shop said it was worthless because of the flaws in it. He wouldn't even take money for it. He just wanted Perkins to say a few words. I left with the pearl in my pocket. Later I heard that a museum was looking for a rose-colored pearl with lots of flaws. I read all about the legend. I figured the pearl belonged in a museum.

"I did the right thing by donating it to the

museum **anonymously.** But after all these years, I wanted to have another look at the pearl. I thought you had found it last night. I didn't even know it was still missing until I read the paper this morning. I came to the hotel to see if I could spot that couple. They looked like the types that would be interested in jewels. I wanted to help find the pearl."

Kira smiled. "You still can. You can come to a meeting tonight."

Barbie gave Captain Sanders the details about the meeting. He agreed to be there.

While they talked, Perkins fluttered down onto a nearby table. He began picking up berries. "One! Two!" he squawked as he delivered two berries into Captain Sanders's pouch.

As they left the captain, Barbie and Kira could hear Perkins still counting. "Clever bird," Kira said. "Now what do we do?"

"Now," Barbie told her, "we tell Kim our plan and hope it works!"

Chapter Seven

After work, Kira met Barbie outside the Art Center. "You look worried," Kira remarked.

"I can't help it," Barbie replied. "If the Whitestones and Captain Sanders are telling the truth, there's only one suspect left."

"Noni!" Kira and Barbie said together.

Barbie pulled out a small notebook. She wrote down the names of all the suspects. "One, two, three," she counted to herself.

Suddenly Barbie stopped counting and looked up. She was remembering what Perkins was squawking after the fire started!

"I think I know what happened!" Barbie whispered.

"What?" Kira begged. "Tell me!"

"Good evening, ladies," a voice behind them interrupted. It was Captain Sanders and Perkins. They were followed by the Whitestones and Noni.

As the suspects arrived, Kim welcomed them inside the center's lobby.

Noni looked around, frowning. "I did not expect to see the others this evening," she said. "I don't understand."

"Please," Barbie began, looking at all their confused faces. "Let me explain why I've asked you to come here tonight. I want to get to the bottom of this mystery."

"That's our hope, too," came a voice from the doorway. It was the police detective in charge of the case. "Thank you for inviting me to the meeting, Barbie. Please continue."

Barbie took a deep breath and began. "I believe I can tell you where the Pink Pearl is." The room went completely silent. "Captain Sanders, would you please empty your pouch onto this table?"

All eyes turned toward the captain. "No problem," he replied confidently. He pulled out a few coins, an old watch, some shriveled berries, a button, a few twigs, and some nuts. When he shook the pouch to make sure it was empty, out rolled the Pink Pearl!

Noni and Kim gasped.

Mrs. Whitestone cried, "I knew it was him all along!"

Barbie put her hand up. "Please, everyone, let me finish. Captain Sanders didn't steal the pearl—"

"Steal it? I didn't even know I had it!" said the captain angrily.

"Then how did it get in his bag?" Noni

wanted to know.

"I'd like to show you that right now," Barbie replied. "Kim, would you please put the wooden box on the refreshment table?"

Barbie then opened the box and placed the pearl inside. Earlier, Kira and Barbie had set up the room exactly as it had looked the night before.

"Everyone may come forward for a closer look," Barbie said. "Please try to take the same positions you were in last night." She stepped aside while the others crowded around the table.

"Now, Captain Sanders," Barbie began, "would you please have Perkins show us his counting trick again?"

"Sure," the confused captain replied. He put his pouch back on and tapped the bird's feet. Everyone in the room watched as Perkins began flapping his big, green wings. The bird began diving at the table, picking up nuts from the bowls. Two by two, he dropped them into the captain's pouch, squawking, "One! Two! Three! Four! Five! Six! Seven! Eight!"

When the bird said "eight," Barbie startled everyone by shouting, "The napkins are on fire!" As the others watched in surprise, she knocked a bowl of nuts onto the floor. Just as before, everyone stepped away from the table as the nuts rolled past them.

"Help!" squawked Perkins. "Nine!"

With the nut bowl empty, Perkins picked up the pearl from the wooden box. He carried it to the captain's pouch and dropped it in!

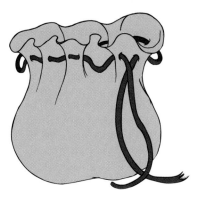

"Well, I'll be!" said the captain, looking at his parrot. "Perkins?" Perkins flapped his wings and squawked, "Captain's pearl!"

"He didn't mean any harm!" Captain Sanders cried. "You're not going to take him away from me, are you?"

The detective put a hand on the captain's arm. "No, Sir," he told him. "Even if we could arrest a bird, something tells me Perkins is too smart to stay locked up for long!"

"Well, one thing is certain," Kira said with a laugh. "If Perkins were locked up, he'd definitely be counting the days until he was free again!"

"Nine! Nine!" Perkins squawked happily as the others laughed.

Kim looked around and sighed. For the first time since the day before, she had a smile on her face. "Now that the Pink Pearl's back, we can have our opening tomorrow night!"

Barbie leaned over to pick up a nut. "Well, we'd better clean up this mess, then!" she chuckled.

The next day, the newspaper headlines read: *Parrot Pockets Pink Pearl!* Thanks to all the publicity, a huge crowd came to the Art Center that night. In honor of the Pink Pearl, many of the guests wore pink—even the Whitestones!

Barbie walked over to an open window. She felt a warm breeze on her face as she gazed out. The last rays of golden sunlight danced on the clear, blue ocean. A small plane cut through a sky filled with puffy, pink clouds.

"Even the sky is dressed for the occasion," Kira said, looking over Barbie's shoulder.

The two friends walked over to Noni, who was getting ready to tell the legend.

"Don't look so worried, Noni. Your storytelling is wonderful," Barbie comforted her.

"It's not that," sighed Noni, with a serious look on her face. "I have been unable to reach my granddaughter by phone today. I hope she's all right."

Just then the museum director stepped up to the microphone. "Ladies and gentlemen, I am proud to introduce one of Hawaii's finest storytellers, Noni Pualani."

Gracefully moving her arms, Noni led a hula. Through song and dance, she told the story of Princess Loki Lani and the Pink Pearl. Then she added the story of Captain Sanders and Perkins.

When the applause died down, Kim spoke. "Thank you, Noni Pualani, for that beautiful story. I would also like to thank some other guests who are with us tonight." She turned toward Captain Sanders. "Thank you, Captain, for finding the Pink Pearl the first time it was lost." The captain touched his cap and smiled as the people clapped.

"And thank you, Barbie and Kira, for finding the pearl the second time," Kim added. The two friends smiled as the crowd applauded.

"I would like to say something," Barbie said, stepping toward the microphone. "Noni Pualani has not told the entire story."

Noni gasped. The crowd went silent.

"As you know," Barbie began, "the Pink

Pearl has mysterious healing powers. Noni had hoped some of those powers would help her granddaughter. And they have." Barbie stepped aside, and a little girl with long, black hair ran into the room.

"Nana Noni!" she cried. "I'm all better now! We flew here today to see you!" Noni hugged her granddaughter tightly. Tears of joy streamed down her face.

The young girl placed a beautiful necklace of flowers around her grandmother's neck. "These are for you, Nana Noni," said the girl. "I hope this pink **lei** is still your favorite."

"Of course," Noni replied. "In flowers, in pearls, and in your healthy cheeks! I love pink."

"I love pink! I love pink!" repeated Perkins.